PREECE, Phil

Nightmare park

Look out for other exciting stories
in the *Shades* series:

SHADES

NIGHTMARE PARK

Philip Preece

Evans

Published by Evans Brothers Limited
2A Portman Mansions
Chiltern St
London W1U 6NR

First published in 2004

British Library Cataloguing in Publication Data
Preece, Phil
Nightmare park. - (Shades)
1. Young adult fiction
I. Title
823. 9'14 [J]

ISBN 023 752730 8

Series Editor: David Orme
Editor: Julia Moffatt
Designer: Rob Walster

Chapter One

It was dark, and Ben was running. His breath came in painful gasps and his side hurt from the effort. As he burst out of the belt of trees he paused, uncertain where to go next.

Ahead of him across the empty winter fields he could see the lights of the fair. It glowed like a fiery city, a blaze of colour in the darkness. Music drifted towards him across the emptiness between.

If only he could get there he'd be safe. But already he could hear his pursuers crashing through the woods behind him. He was no wimp, but there were three of them: Masters, Lee and Danny. They were well-known bullies who always picked on people when they were alone.

He looked again at the dark empty fields stretching ahead of him. He wasn't sure if he could make it.

'Oi, come on, he's here!'

The shout came from somewhere behind him. It sounded frighteningly near. Like a shot he was off running again.

This was the very edge of the park; nobody came here, usually. It was hard going, with long grass dragging at his feet.

Behind him he could hear the hunters' heavy footsteps. They weren't shouting now. They were silent, angry, saving their breath for running, determined to get their prey. Gradually they were gaining on him. He thought he could hear their tense breathing, almost feel it on the back of his neck.

Then with a last desperate spurt he left them behind. He burst between the dark backs of two wagons and at once he was among the bright lights and noise of the fair with its crowds of people.

He pushed through the crowd urgently. He had to get away, as far away from them as possible. He had to lose himself in the fair.

Everywhere people were shouting and smiling, out to have a good time. Some of them held balloons and fluffy monkeys they'd won on the stalls. Groups of girls waltzed by with their arms linked together and lads were pushing each other and laughing. Now he was surrounded by people, but Ben had never felt so much alone. What if his pursuers caught him? Would anybody try to stop them, even in this crowd? He didn't think so. He turned blindly on, desperate to put as much distance as possible between himself and his tormentors.

People were screaming with excitement as they whirled around on the rides. Multi-coloured lights flashed on and off in time to the loud music that was blasting out.

He hurried on through the fair. Everyone around him seemed to be having a good time. There was no sign yet of anyone following him. Surely they'd never find him in this crowd, would they?

Gradually he began to relax. He wandered on more slowly now. He'd stay in the fair for a while, he decided, till he was sure he was safe, then make his way home.

At last Ben found he'd wandered right though the fair. At its farthest edge he saw a brightly-lit sideshow with a crowd in front of it. *Dreamland*, it said in lights. Tall gas jets flared on either side of a small stage.

A man in a black tailcoat was calling out, 'Roll up, roll up. Don't miss the chance of a lifetime. See your dreams come true. We have the very latest machinery. We can show your innermost secret thoughts.'

Just then a girl came out of a door at the back of the stage; she was smiling and excited. She waved to her waiting friends.

'I saw it!' she screamed. 'My secret dream!' Her friends giggled.

Ben felt himself being pushed forward to the front of the surging crowd. Suddenly he was being pressed against the stage. The man in black smiled and reached down a hand to lift him clear.

'Come on,' he said. 'You'll be safe up here.'

At that moment Ben noticed a movement out of the corner of his eye. Masters and the others had reached the back of the crowd where he had been standing just a minute ago. They'd got him now. Everyone could see him as he stood up there on the stage.

'Well done,' said the showman loudly, with a smile. He had a black moustache and dark, laughing eyes. 'Here's a young man who wants to see his dreams come true. Not afraid, are you?'

As if from nowhere a beautiful assistant

appeared and took his hand. She was wearing a flame-red dress.

'Look after the gentleman would you, Lola?' said the showman. Lola smiled at them both.

Ben allowed her to lead him across the stage. But instead of going through the tinselled door at the back, he found himself being ushered towards another door off to one side which he hadn't noticed before.

Suddenly Ben felt uneasy. At once the showman was beside him.

'The main door's only for ordinary people,' he whispered. 'This one's special. It's for people who dare to take a chance. People who actually want to make their dreams come true.'

Ben wasn't sure. He didn't want anyone to think he was a coward.

As he hesitated, he looked over his

shoulder. Masters, Lee and Danny were pushing their way forward through the crowd.

'A special door,' repeated the showman, 'for people like you. If you dare.'

With a last nervous glance back at the bullies, Ben let himself be led through the doorway into the blackness inside.

Chapter Two

At first he could see nothing. Everything was in total darkness.

Ben felt himself being guided to a cushioned chair. The showman's hand gripped his shoulder tightly. Confused, he sat still for a moment. Then suddenly a bank of TV screens jumped into life.

'Now!' said the showman.

Ben saw himself as he had been a few minutes ago, hurrying across the fields followed by the louts. He watched in amazement as his face was shown in a huge close-up. He was looking worried, frightened even.

'How…?' he began.

'Watch,' said the showman.

Then he was at school, spread large across the screens. He was in class, and the teacher was telling him off. He remembered that day. He'd come bottom in the test.

'There's no excuse,' the teacher was saying. 'You're bone idle. It's either that or sheer stupidity, getting these low marks.'

The class laughed.

Ben watched his own face in close-up. He looked as if he might be going to cry. He saw the faces of his classmates, one after another. One or two of the boys were sneering. There was a girl's face laughing at him.

This time Ben said nothing.

The picture changed, and he was at the disco. He remembered that too. He was standing on his own. Everyone else was having a good time. He watched himself in despair as he walked across and asked a girl to dance. He saw her expression before she turned away to giggle with her friends.

He squirmed with shame as he relived the moment. He'd been really stupid. After all, it was Lisa, the best-looking girl in the school. He'd never had a chance in the first place.

The lights came on slowly. The show seemed to be over. Ben hoped no one could see his burning face. He'd watched

his worst nightmare – and it was true.
He jumped up quickly. He couldn't wait
to get out of there.

'Not a pretty sight was it?' asked
the showman.

Ben had to agree. He'd never realised
before just how much of a joke he
was. He'd never guessed he looked
as bad as that.

'But now we have something very special
to show you. Because here at Dreamland
we have an incredible new process. It really
can make all your dreams come true!'

As he spoke the lovely assistant came
over and smiled kindly at Ben. She helped
him back into his chair and patted his
arm gently.

The lights dimmed once again. The
screens showed the classroom once more,
but this time what happened was completely

different. The teacher was giving out the test results, and she was just coming to Ben's name. But when she reached it, Ben could hardly believe what she was saying. This time he was top of the class!

He saw the amazed expressions of his classmates, and heard the teacher telling him how clever he was. The whole class was applauding. The sound roared in his ears, echoing louder and louder.

Then the action switched to another scene. Lisa, the girl he liked, the one who had turned away and laughed at him at the dance, was coming up to him. She was telling him how great it was that he'd come top of the class. She was smiling at him. Her friends were smiling at him too.

He caught the expressions on the faces of one or two of the boys. It was sheer envy. For once he was a success!

The scene shifted and he recognised the school grounds. The bullies were there and he watched them head towards him in front of everyone. He winced, sure of what was going to happen.

The next thing he knew, Masters was flat on his back with a surprised expression on his face. He was looking very stupid. Everyone was laughing. The other two were running off.

One or two of the lads were slapping him on the back.

'Well done,' they were saying. 'Well done, well done, well done...'

Ben blinked as the lights came up.

'That's how it could be, Ben,' the showman was saying. 'We can make your secret dreams come true.'

'Really?' asked Ben. He wanted this. He wanted to be what he'd seen on the screen, instead of being the boy he really was.

'What do I have to do?' Suddenly he had a moment of doubt. He wasn't stupid. 'What's the catch?' he asked.

'Absolutely no catch,' said the man. 'We're here to make people's dreams come true. There's just a small management charge to cover overheads. Nothing you can't afford.'

'How much?' asked Ben doubtfully. After all, he hadn't got a job. He was still at school. He didn't even have a paper round.

'The charge for making each dream come true? Oh, just a few minutes of your time.'

It didn't seem like much.

'Yes, just a few short minutes of time. You've got your whole life in front of you. You'll never miss a minute here and there.'

19

'But what do you want with them?'

'Oh, let's just say we find them very useful.' As the man spoke the screens came on again. There, smiling from them all was one huge picture of Ben.
He was happy, triumphant.

He thought of Lisa smiling back at him.

'OK,' he said. 'What do I have to do?'

'Just sign here.'

The beautiful assistant came over, slowly, smiling, carrying a huge book. She held it open in front of Ben. There was a strange pen, like a long feather with a sharp nib.

'Careful,' said the showman, 'it's sharp. Oh, too late.'

Ben felt a searing pain.

'Ow!' he shouted.

He'd cut his finger on the nib.

'Never mind, just sign here and it'll all be over in a moment.'

He pointed to a dotted line at the bottom of the page. It was made of some stiff, thick paper and covered in strange, old-fashioned writing.

Ben signed his name carefully on the line. He was startled to see that the ink was as red as blood.

'There,' he said.

The showman slapped the book shut with a snap.

'Thank you,' he said.

'Is that it?' asked Ben.

'Oh yes, that's it.' The showman laughed, showing long white teeth. For a moment he made Ben think of a wolf.

He felt himself being eased out of his seat and towards the door. The showman's sharp fingers gripped his shoulder almost painfully.

As the lights of the fair blazed out again Ben felt suddenly nervous. For some reason the hand felt just like a claw.

Chapter Three

The next day Ben went to school as normal. Last night seemed like a dream. He wasn't sure whether it had been a good dream or not.

He'd forgotten all about it by the last period of the day. There'd been a test in Maths the day before. The teacher was reading out the marks. Ben wasn't really

paying attention. He knew he hadn't done enough work for it. But he was in for a surprise. It was just like in the vision.
He had actually scored the top mark!

Everything seemed to spin around him. People were turning round and smiling at him. The teacher was congratulating him, just like he'd seen on the TV screens. Then the whole class was applauding.

After school he couldn't wait to get home. One or two of his classmates slapped him on the back on the way out of school. He ran home as fast as he could. He burst into the house, shouting.

His mother came out of the kitchen.

'Guess what!' he said. 'I came top in the test!'

Mum didn't say anything.

'Everyone was clapping,' he said. 'It was great!'

She still hadn't said anything. He looked at her more closely. Her eyes were red. It looked as if she'd been crying.

'What's the matter?' he asked.

'It's Jip.'

Jip was Ben's dog. Ben had had him since he was a puppy.

'There's been an accident. He was knocked down by a car. I can't think how he got out on to the road.'

All Ben's high spirits suddenly drained away. He was hardly listening to what his mother had to say. The dog was at the vet's.

'Is he going to be all right?'

'They weren't sure.' His mother put a hand on his arm. 'The vet thinks we ought to be ready for the worst.'

Ben was silent. Only a minute ago he'd been on top of the world. But a lot can happen in a minute.

Ben felt depressed for the rest of
the evening.

The next day at lunchtime as Ben went
out on to the school field he saw a sight
he'd been dreading. The three bullies were
coming towards him.

Masters came right up to him, jeering.

'You thought you'd got away with it the
other night, didn't you?' he said sneeringly.
'Well, your luck's just run out, kid!'

He poked Ben hard in the chest. His
other hand was already clenched into
a hard fist. Lee and Danny sniggered.
Everyone was looking by this time.

Ben wasn't sure exactly what happened,
but the next thing he knew Masters was
lying flat on his back gasping for breath.
He looked really surprised. Everybody burst
out laughing.

Lee and Danny's mouths dropped open.
Masters was the hardest kid in the whole
school. Next minute they ran off. Masters
jumped to his feet and sped off after
them. Everybody clustered around Ben,
congratulating him. It was great. He
was a hero, even if he hadn't actually
done anything.

Still, it felt good being popular. *Really*
good. He glowed all the way through
afternoon school.

On the way home Ben remembered Jip.
He hoped his dog was going to be all right.

When he got back he had a surprise.
Dad was there. He and Mum were in the
living room. Dad didn't usually come home
till late. They sat silent, Dad looking grim.
Ben felt his heart jump in his chest.

'We've had some bad news,' said Mum.

'Is it – Jip?'

'No. He's still at the vet's. There's been no change. It's your dad. He's lost his job.'

Ben looked at his dad. He sat at the table with his head bowed. He looked stunned.

It was quiet in the house that night. Everyone was depressed. Ben had a lot to think about. He went to bed early but lay awake for hours worrying about the bargain he had made at Dreamland.

A few minutes of time hadn't seemed like a high price to pay for having his dreams come true, at least not the way the showman told it. But a lot could happen in a minute. Now it seemed that for every good thing, something bad had to happen.

Getting things you hadn't worked for was really cheating, he could see that now. He dreaded to think what might happen next.

He was just leaving school the next day when a girl came up to him.

'Hello,' she said. It was Lisa, the best-looking girl in the school, the one he'd liked all along. He'd wanted to go out with her ever since he'd first seen her. He remembered the time she'd turned him down at the dance.

'I loved the way you stood up to those yobs,' she said. 'They've been getting away with it for far too long.' She was looking at Ben as if she really liked him.

Ben felt a chill running down his spine. It was all happening just like he'd been shown it in Dreamland. He turned away, suddenly scared of what might happen next. This time he was really afraid to go home.

Chapter Four

When Ben got back his mother wasn't there. His dad was.

'Where's Mum?' he asked.

'She's had to go to the hospital,' Dad said.

Ben felt as if a bony hand was slowly squeezing his heart.

'It's your grandma. She's very ill.

They're not sure…' Dad didn't finish
the sentence.

Ben felt his stomach turn over. He
knew now that something was very
wrong, something to do with Dreamland.
The dream was turning out to be a
nightmare. He wondered where it was
all going to end.

He tried to shut out the thoughts that
were coming to him. Ever since he'd signed
the book his dreams had come true, just as
he'd been promised. But then terrible things
had happened as well: the dog, his dad's
job, and now Grandma.

He could have come top by studying –
he realised that now. He could have really
stood up to the bullies. He'd seen how
easy it was. Maybe Lisa really liked him.
Perhaps it was easier to be a success than
he knew.

But now he was afraid of what might happen next. He didn't want any more good luck. He wished he could go back and start all over again.

A desperate thought came to him. He had to go back to the fair, back to Dreamland. Somehow he had to cancel the contract. Otherwise he didn't like to think about the price for his next piece of good luck.

After tea Dad announced it was time for them to go to the hospital.

But Ben couldn't get the thought of the bargain out of his mind. He felt terrible about Grandma's illness. It was all his fault. If he hadn't gone to Dreamland in the first place she would still be all right. He had to stop what was happening. Now, right away. He had to see the showman and explain. If Ben could only persuade him to cancel the

contract, then all these terrible things
would stop.

'I can't go,' he said. 'I – I've got too
much homework to do.'

Dad glanced at him sharply.

'But your grandma's ill,' he said. 'This
is serious. I'm surprised you can't spare
the time to see if she's all right. And
there's your mum. She'll want to see
you. Leave the homework for now.
It can't be all that important.'

'It is,' said Ben desperately. 'I've got
do it for tomorrow. I've promised. I'll
be in trouble if I don't. It should have
been in last week.'

Now Dad was starting to look annoyed.

'Well, I don't know,' he began, but just
then he caught sight of the clock. 'I can't
think what your mother's going to say,'
he said. 'Anyway I can't stop here talking.

Somebody's got to go and see if they're both all right.'

He threw Ben a suspicious glance, as if he knew Ben was up to something. Luckily for Ben, he went anyway and Ben found himself alone.

He breathed a deep sigh of relief. His dad was always telling him what to do. None of his friends got this kind of treatment. It made him really cross sometimes – the way they treated him like a kid. But there was no time to worry about that now. At last he could carry out his plan to make everything all right. He waited until he heard the sound of the car pulling away, then straight away he grabbed his coat.

It was dark outside. He set off at a run. The sooner he got to the fair, the sooner he'd be back. If he wasn't back by the time

Mum and Dad got home he really would be in trouble. But with any luck the showman would see sense about the deal, and all this trouble would be sorted out. Then Jip would be all right, Grandma would recover and Dad could get another job. He hurried on towards the fair.

When he reached it the crowds were there as usual. People were screaming as they whirled around on the rides, but now they didn't sound as if they were enjoying themselves. To Ben they sounded more as if they were being frightened half to death.

He searched the fair anxiously, looking for Dreamland. It seemed to be taking forever. And then at last he found it, right on the farthest side. But at once he could see that something was terribly wrong. There were no lights on the stage. Dreamland didn't seem to be open. And

when he looked closely, it seemed as if
it had been closed for a very long time.
The paint was peeling, light bulbs in the
Dreamland sign were missing, and some
of the steps had rotted away completely.
The main entrance was all boarded up.
How could it have got so run down in
such a short time?

It was quiet here at the edge of the fair.
Ben suddenly felt cold. He turned, looking
for someone to help him. Nearby was a
small stall with games and prizes. The
man running it was just closing up.

'Excuse me,' said Ben. 'What's happened
to Dreamland?' The man looked at him as if
he was mad, then shrugged and turned away.

Ben felt a shiver of fear. How was he
going to end the contract now?

He had to see the man in black, somehow.
If not, there was only one way left. It was a

long shot, but Ben had no choice. He had to get his hands on that contract. He would come back later when no one was around. He was going to have to break in.

All the lights were on in the house when he got back. Ben's heart sank. He must have been at the fair longer than he'd thought. As he opened the door he could hear Dad's voice sounding angry.

'Telling us lies,' he was saying. 'That's what makes it worse.'

Ben pushed open the living room door. Dad swung round.

'Where do you think you've been?' he shouted. He didn't wait for an answer. 'We've been worried sick. I thought you had some homework to do?'

Ben looked across at Mum. She was sitting at the table with her head in her hands.

'Where have you been at this time of night?' shouted his dad again.

Ben took a deep breath.

'I've been to the fair,' he began, but before he could explain his dad interrupted.

'The fair? You've been to the fair? Out enjoying yourself with your grandma in hospital? Look at you. You couldn't care less about anybody but yourself!'

It wasn't true – he did care about everyone else. But – how could he begin to explain?

Ben opened his mouth to speak but no words came out. He wanted to tell them that he'd been trying to help everybody, trying to stop everything from going wrong. But how could he tell them about Dreamland and the bargain that he'd made?

But Dad wasn't finished.

'Well that's it,' he was saying. 'We've been too soft with you lately. From now on, you're grounded.'

Grounded? Ben opened his mouth to protest. He couldn't be grounded. He had to get back to the fair. He had to make everything all right again. He had to see the showman.

'Listen,' he began.

But what could he say? How could he tell them he was trying to save them from the terrible things that had happened, and maybe even worse things to come?

For the first time since Ben had come in his mother raised her head. She looked straight at him. The expression on her face pierced his heart. If only he could make them understand. Sadly he turned and went out of the room.

There was only one thing for it. He'd have to wait until everyone was asleep. Then he would make one final attempt to get back into Dreamland.

He had one last chance before it was too late.

Chapter Five

Ben lay silently in the dark and waited
until his parents were safely in bed and
everything was quiet. Then as quietly
as he could, he let himself out of the
house into the black winter night.
The fields were deserted. He could
just make out the shadowy shape of
the fair in the darkness.

When he reached the fair all the rides were closed up. The whole place was deserted. The contrast with the normal light and noise was eerie. He felt as if he was being watched from the blank shuttered stalls and darkened rides.

At last he reached Dreamland. His footsteps sounded loud as he walked up the rotting steps. He had brought a hammer with him, and he started to prise the boards away from the door. They resisted, then gave way with a terrible wrenching noise that sounded as loud as an explosion in the night.

Inside it was pitch dark. Ben stepped forward uncertainly. A flame sprang up in front of him. Then another, and another, until Ben was surrounded by a ring of flames. A laugh like stones sliding down a hillside came out of the shadows. It was the man in black.

'Ah, Ben,' he said. 'So you have found us. Welcome. What can we do for you?'

'I – I want my contract back.'

'But Ben, we made a bargain.'

'I know. But—'

'Didn't you get what you were promised?'

'Yes. But—' Ben wanted to say it hadn't been fair but somehow he just couldn't find the right words.

'You signed, Ben. Look.'

As the man spoke the light increased. In the middle of the room Ben could see there was a wide round pit. Out of it smoke or steam was rising, lit by a fiery glow from underneath. A steep flight of stairs went straight down into its depths.

As he watched, Lola came slowly up the stairs wreathed in coils of smoke. She was smiling, holding the book with the contract in. Her crimson dress looked as if it were on fire. She handed the book to the showman and went back down the stairs.

Now the man in black was opening the book. He flicked through the huge pages. Ben could see that there were dozens of agreements similar to his own.

'Where is it? Ah, yes, here.' He held the book open for Ben to see. 'There you are. That is your signature isn't it?'

'Yes, but—'

He made as if to close the book.

In that moment Ben knew what he had to do. With a desperate lunge he reached for the book. His fingers grabbed the edge of the parchment and held on. He had to get it. He had to rip out the page with his signature on it.

But the showman was tugging back. For a moment they teetered on the edge of the pit. Flames flared up from the depths below.

Ben held on to the page for grim life. He was being pulled nearer and nearer to the flames. His hold on the page was the only thing between him and oblivion. He felt the page beginning to tear. Ben gave one last desperate tug. It ripped straight across.

The man in black hung for a moment over the edge of the hole. With a despairing cry he fell backwards into the fiery pit. Flames shot up to the ceiling, followed by a demonic howl of fury.

Ben looked down in horror. The man in black was gone, taking the book and the contract with him. Now he would never be free.

The flames rose up above his head. Smoke swirled around him, filling the room. He took a step backwards, trying to feel his way towards to the door. The whole place was becoming an inferno. He scrabbled for the exit, stumbling forward now. Where was it? He didn't want to die. Smoke and flames were everywhere. He was choking to death.

Then Ben felt himself falling, falling, falling....

Chapter Six

Ben found himself wandering in a maze. Everything was dark. Far ahead he thought he saw a light. The light grew brighter. He went nearer to it. He heard a voice speaking his name, over and over. He opened his eyes.

He was lying on the cold damp ground outside. Daylight streamed into his eyes. It was morning.

In front of him the embers of what was once Dreamland still glowed. As he watched, the roof caved in with a huge shower of sparks. Somehow he had managed to stagger out just in the nick of time.

He could see the orange flashing lights of fire engines and firemen aiming hosepipes, trying to stop the fire spreading to the other stalls and caravans. People were standing anxiously in groups.

Then Mum was there, and Dad with her. Dad was looking angry. Mum just looked relieved. They must have come looking for him when they found he wasn't in bed.

'How dare you...?' began Dad.

'Not now,' said Mum.

'How did you find me?' asked Ben.

'When we saw that your bed hadn't been slept in, we guessed you must have come here,' said Mum. 'I'm just glad you're safe.'

Together they stood and watched the fire destroying Dreamland for ever.

'We've got some good news for you,' said Mum. 'I've just phoned the hospital. Gran's out of danger. She's going to be OK.'

'And the vet rang. Jip's coming home today,' said Dad.

'But the best news is Dad's getting his old job back. They phoned this morning,' said Mum, looking pleased.

'Not just my old job,' said Dad. 'The firm's expanding. They've given me a better job, with more money.'

He looked at Ben.

'It seems like our luck has changed,' he said. He was smiling for the first time in days.

Ben looked down. He was holding something screwed up tightly in his hand.

It was a strip of charred parchment torn from the bottom of a page. His name was written on it in faded red ink. As he watched, it crumpled into ash and blew away in the early morning light.

A group of his friends on their way to school came up to watch the end of the fire. Lisa was with them.

'You're safe,' she said. 'I am glad.' She gave him a hug.

Ben heaved a huge sigh of relief. Everything was going to be all right.

'Time to go home,' said Mum.

They turned away. All that was left of Dreamland was a heap of smoking ash.

It was the last night of the fair. Ben had gone along with Lisa and his other friends for some last-minute fun. He had taken some persuading, but now he was really enjoying himself. It was great. He could enjoy the fair now he had nothing to worry about.

They went on all the rides, laughing and shouting. They ate candyfloss and won coconuts and toys.

Just as they were leaving Ben spotted something between the stalls that made him rub his eyes. He wandered over towards it to get a clearer view.

Dreamland, said the lights of the sideshow. As he watched in amazement, he recognised the man in black. He had his hand on a boy's shoulder. With another shock Ben realised it was Masters. He was being led towards a little door at the side of the stage.

Ben was too far away to be sure but he could have sworn the man looked straight at him. His smile seemed to say, 'No hard feelings.' Masters was smiling too as he went through the door.

Ben shuddered.

The man in black laughed, showing his long, wolf-like teeth. This time Ben got the message loud and clear.

'There are always people around who like a bargain,' it said. 'We sign them up at Dreamland every day.'

Look out for this exciting story
in the *Shades* series:

Tears of a Friend

Joanna Kenrick

Next day is Saturday. There's a new
shopping centre near me. It's got Top Shop
and Miss Selfridge and all the really good
high-street stores. There are some funky
little boutiques too. You can find really
unusual stuff in them: camouflage clothes
and flares. We've been coming here since
it opened a few months ago and I always
spend too much money. Not that I get
much of an allowance.

I look around at the crowds of people.

The centre is always packed on a Saturday.

'Over here, Cassie!' calls Claire. She is looking stunning as usual. Pink crop-top and tight jeans. And—

'Oh my God!' I gasp. 'Have you had your belly-button pierced?'

'Fooled you!' giggles Claire. She shows me the little sparkly jewel. 'It's stick-on. I bought it just now. Claire's Accessories.' She winks. 'So good they named it after me!'

'It looks really cool,' I say. Now I want one too. But that would be copying. And my tummy isn't flat like hers. Maybe if I don't have dinner tonight?

'Come on, there's some new stuff in Top Shop.' Claire drags me off.

We have a brilliant time. I love trying on clothes. Dresses, trousers, little tops, big baggy jumpers, short skirts – it's how I imagine heaven to be. One big

shopping centre in the sky where you
can shop forever.

We're in Dorothy Perkins. Claire has got
this dress on that looks amazing. (Of course.
I mean, she could wear a dustbin sack and
look amazing.)

I'm pulling on a dark green velvet top. I
gasp at myself in the mirror. I look *fantastic*.
The top is very low cut. I have a cleavage.

I turn to Claire. 'What do you think?'

'Hang on a minute,' she says. 'Do you
think this makes me look fat?'

'No,' I say, 'but look at me!'

She glances at me. 'It's all right.'

She's looking at herself again.

I'm suddenly angry. 'Look properly!'
I say loudly.

Claire looks surprised. And a bit
annoyed. But she *does* look at me.

'Yeah, it's nice. Bit revealing though,

isn't it? For you, I mean.'

'What do you mean, for me?'

I can feel hot, red anger boiling up inside me.

'Well,' Claire shrugs, 'it's just not your style.'

I am furious now.

'And what exactly is my style? Looking boring, I suppose? Being covered up? Wearing last year's fashions? Wearing the cheap versions of *your* clothes? Oh, *I* know what my style is. It's just anything worse than yours. To make you look better when you stand next to me. Well thanks a lot!'

As I pull the green top over my head I hear a seam rip. I don't care.

'See you around, Claire,' I say. She looks really silly, her mouth hanging open as she stares at me. I storm out of the changing room. I fling the top at the shop assistant.

'No thanks,' I say. 'It's not my *style*.'

What an exit!

I am very impressed with myself. To start with. But after about five minutes I begin to feel really down. When I get home I burst into tears. I'm angry with myself and with Claire. After a while I'm not angry any more, just sad.

Maybe I can make it up with Claire tomorrow? But why should I? She should say sorry first.

I fall asleep with a headache.

Blitz - David Orme

It's World War II and Martin has been
evacuated to the country. He hates it so much,
he runs back home to London. But home isn't
where it used to be...

Gateway from Hell - John Banks

Lisa and her friends are determined to stop the
new road being built. Especially as it means
digging up Mott Hill. Because something
ancient lies beneath the hill. Something
dangerous - something *deadly*...

A Murder of Crows - Penny Bates

Ben is new to the country, and when he makes
friends with a lonely crow, finds himself being
bullied. Now the bullies want him to hurt his
only friend. But they have reckoned without
the power of crow law...

Hunter's Moon - John Townsend

Neil loves working as a gamekeeper. But something very strange is going on in the woods… What is the meaning of the message Neil receives? And why should he beware the Hunter's Moon?

Nightmare Park - Philip Preece

Dreamland – a place where your dreams come true.
Ben thinks it's a joke at first. But he'd give anything to be popular. Losing a few short minutes of his life, seems a small price to pay. But a lot can happen in a minute. And Ben soon realises nothing in life should be this easy…

Plague - David Orme

The year is 1665 and plague has come to the city of London. For Henry Harper, life will never be the same. His father is dead, and his mother and brother have fled to the country. Now Henry is alone, and must find a way to escape from the city he loves, before he, too, is struck down...

Space Explorers - David Johnson

Sammi and Zak have been stranded on a strange planet, surrounded by deadly spear plants. Luckily mysterious horned-creatures rescue them. Now all they need to do is get back to their ship...

Tears of a Friend - Joanna Kenrick

Cassie and Claire have been friends *for ever*.
Cassie thinks nothing will ever split them
apart. But then, the unthinkable happens.
They have a row, and now Cassie feels so
alone. What can she do to mend a friendship?
Or has she lost Claire – for good?

Treachery by Night - Ann Ruffell

Glencoe, 1692
Conn longs to be a brave warrior, just like his
cousin Jamie. But what kind of warrior has a
withered arm? Then he finds a sword in the
heather, and he learns to fight using his good
arm. And when the treacherous Campbells
bring Redcoats into the Macdonald valley,
Conn is going to need all the strength he
can muster...